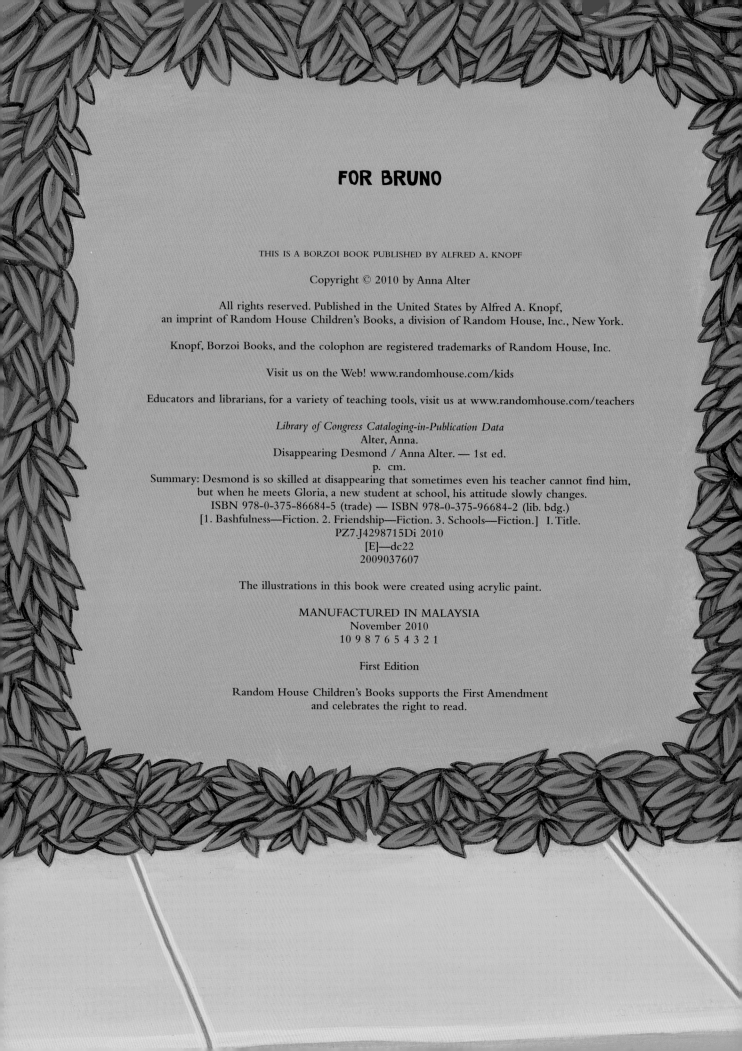

FOR BRUNO

THIS IS A BORZOI BOOK PUBLISHED BY ALFRED A. KNOPF

Visit us on the Web! www.randomhouse.com/kids

Educators and librarians, for a variety of teaching tools, visit us at www.randomhouse.com/teachers

Library of Congress Cataloging-in-Publication Data
Alter, Anna.
Disappearing Desmond / Anna Alter. — 1st ed.
p. cm.
Summary: Desmond is so skilled at disappearing that sometimes even his teacher cannot find him,
but when he meets Gloria, a new student at school, his attitude slowly changes.
ISBN 978-0-375-86684-5 (trade) — ISBN 978-0-375-96684-2 (lib. bdg.)
[1. Bashfulness—Fiction. 2. Friendship—Fiction. 3. Schools—Fiction.] I. Title.
PZ7.J4298715Di 2010
[E]—dc22
2009037607

The illustrations in this book were created using acrylic paint.

MANUFACTURED IN MALAYSIA
November 2010
10 9 8 7 6 5 4 3 2 1

First Edition

Random House Children's Books supports the First Amendment
and celebrates the right to read.

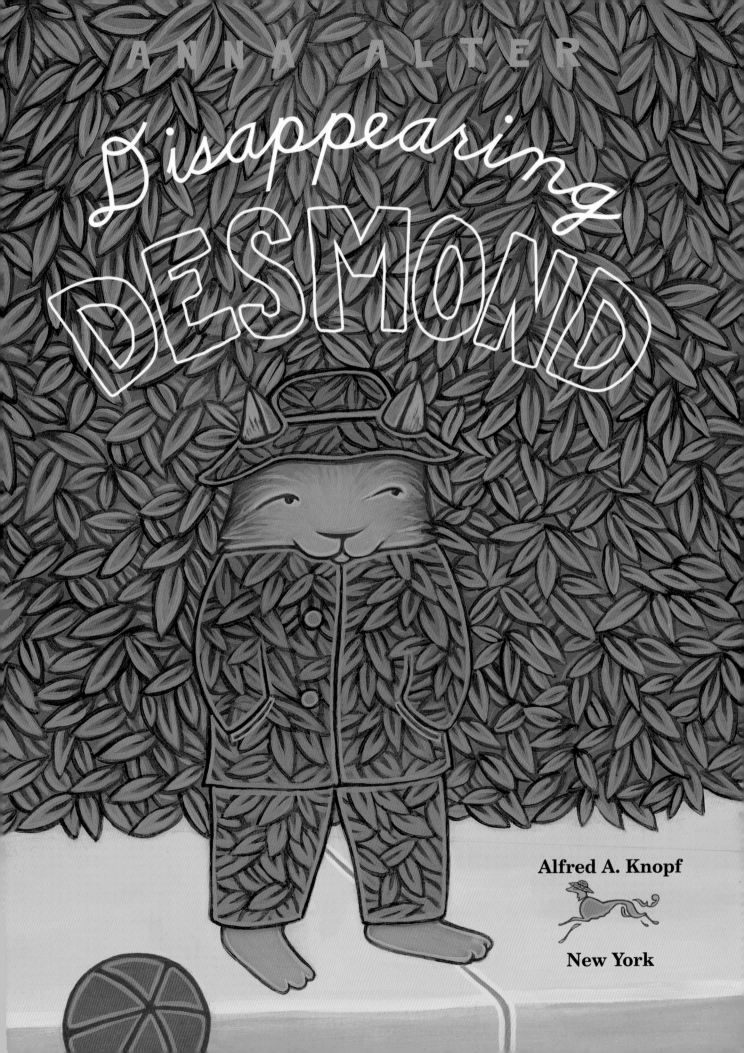

ANNA ALTER

Disappearing
DESMOND

Alfred A. Knopf

New York

Desmond was very hard to spot
in an art museum.

No one could find him at the beach

or on a snowy day.

Desmond liked to disappear.

His family was the same way.

At school, Desmond hid
during library hour,

at lunchtime,

and at recess.

He was always prepared for field trips.

Sometimes, even his teacher could not find him.

Then one day someone new came to school.

Her name was Gloria and she liked to be noticed.

Before long, a strange thing happened.

Desmond froze. He couldn't believe it. No one had ever seen him when he was hiding before.

After school, it happened again.

It happened over,

and over,

and over again.

Until one morning Gloria walked right up to him.
"Hi, Desmond," she said. "You are reading my
favorite book. May I join you?"

Gloria and Desmond read together all morning long.

The next day, Gloria taught Desmond how to play King of the Castle.

Desmond taught Gloria how to hide from bandits.

They played together every day.

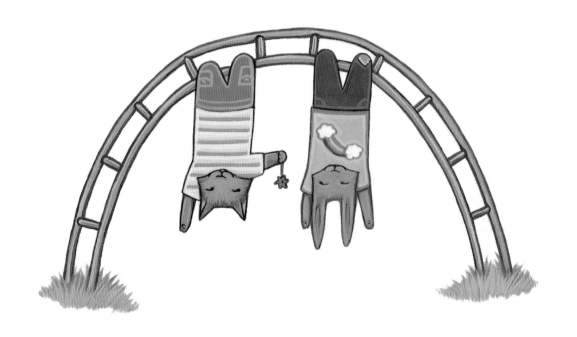

On Monday morning when he came to school,
Desmond felt different. He looked different, too.

He couldn't remember why he ever
wanted to disappear in the first place.

Neither could his family.

Then one afternoon on the playground,
Desmond heard a sound in the bushes.

He went to take a closer look.

The boy in the bushes couldn't believe it.
No one had ever seen him when
he was hiding before.

Desmond, Gloria, and Harold spent the rest of
the afternoon playing kickball on the playground.
Soon everyone joined in the fun.

That is, almost everyone.